The Adventures of Celtic:
The Long Journey Home

Todd Hveem

Todd Hveem

AuthorHouse™
1663 Liberty Drive
Bloomington, IN 47403
www.authorhouse.com
Phone: 1 (800) 839-8640

Published by AuthorHouse 02/09/2015

ISBN: 978-1-4969-6908-8 (sc)
ISBN: 978-1-4969-6909-5 (e)

Library of Congress Control Number: 2015902023

Any people depicted in stock imagery provided by Thinkstock are models,
and such images are being used for illustrative purposes only.
Certain stock imagery © Thinkstock.

This book is printed on acid-free paper.

Because of the dynamic nature of the Internet, any web addresses or links contained in this book may have changed
since publication and may no longer be valid. The views expressed in this work are solely those of the author and do not
necessarily reflect the views of the publisher, and the publisher hereby disclaims any responsibility for them.

CHAPTER 1

When all of the dogs were outside of the dog pound, I felt this great sense of accomplishment. In fact, for a long time, I just looked around and smiled.

There was a basset hound running in one direction, a poodle running in the other and two German Shepherds chasing each other like Bugs Bunny and Elmer Fudd in that cartoon Tyler and I always watch.

"Wow," I thought to myself. "I can't believe how happy these dogs are to be free."

I took a deep breath and smiled. I just knew I should receive some type of "Dog of the Year" award for what I had just pulled off.

Then it hit me. Tyler was not there. My Grandpa was not there. Dad and "The Mama" were at home. And Colton was probably out with his friends.

I, Celtic, had just let 100 dogs out of the pound. But not one of us knew how to get home.

"Hey, little one," barked a big Irish setter named Leprechaun. "Thanks for letting us out. But do you know where I live? Which way do I need to go to get back to my house?"

"Yea, Jose," said a Chihuahua named Taco. "I need to find my casa, man. I am late for a big fiesta. Take me to my crib, Jose."

All of the sudden I started to sweat. What had I done? I got all of the dogs out. But now they had nowhere to go.

"Just sit tight, guys," I told the group, which was getting mighty restless. "I will think of something."

I had nothing. All I wanted to do was run. But if I ran, everybody would run after me. And, sooner or later, they would realize I was just as lost as they were.

"C'mon, man," said Bruiser, a big bulldog who had a serious sinus infection. "Surely, you have a plan. Don't tell me you got us out and now are going to leave us high and dry."

"No, way," I said. "I will get us to a safe place and then we are all going to have to follow our nose."

Just then, I looked into the pack and saw another dog that looked just like me. Then, I turned around and there was another dog that looked just like the other dog.

I knew my family was different than me. They were, well, humans. But I never thought much about my dog family. In fact, I didn't even realize I might have a dog family.

CHAPTER 2

I immediately went over to the first dog and started sniffing his entire body.

"Say," he said. "What are you doing?"

I didn't pay any attention. This dog looked almost identical to me. And I wanted to figure out why.

"Hey, dude," the dog said again. "What are you doing?"

I finally gave in.

"I am trying to figure out why you look so much like me," I said. "And that other dog, over there. She looks like both of us."

The almost-identical looking Welsh Terrier turned his head and nodded to the other puppy. She came running over to both of us.

"This," said the dog I was sniffing, "is my sister. We live together."

I couldn't believe it.

"How did you both get caught by the Dog Catcher at once?" I asked.

"Our Mom let us outside and we thought it would be fun to sneak out of the back yard," the young girl said with a shy giggle.

"Yea," the brother added. "We were playing chase around the entire neighborhood when we ran into the Dog Catcher."

I started to remember when the Dog Catcher almost caught the Hidden Lake Hounds when we went to see Grandma. It was very scary.

But these two didn't seem scared at all. They seemed like they had known each other all their lives.

"When we were just eight-weeks old, our family adopted both of us," the boy dog said. "We have never been apart. We fight sometimes, but we always do everything together."

I had to admit, it would be nice to have a dog playmate instead of three fleabags to chase around the house.

"We have a big back yard," the girl dog said. "We also have a swimming pool. We take turns diving off the diving board."

Now, I was really getting jealous.

"But do you have a 9-year-old boy to play with?" I asked.

They both hung their head.

"No," they both said at once. "That is why we are always together."

I knew Tyler was a special guy. But this made me realize it even more.

"What are your names?" I asked.

"I am Shaq," the boy dog blurted out.

"And I am Kobe," said his twin sister. "Our parents are big Lakers' fans."

Wow, I thought. We don't like the Lakers in my house. But I sure like these two.

"My family likes the Celtics," I said. "That is why they named me Celtic."

They both laughed. They knew who I was right from the start.

"You are our brother," Kobe said. "Our parents were named Boston and L.A. You, obviously, took after Boston."

"But how did you know I was your brother?" I asked.

"Everybody knows you, Celtic," Shaq said. "You are famous. When we saw how much you looked like us, we figured it had to be you."

For the first time in my life, I couldn't speak. I couldn't even bark. I just whimpered and cried. I was so happy. I loved Shaq and Kobe. I wanted to be with them.

"Hey, three amigos," Taco said from the middle of a huge pack of dogs. "I think I hear the owner of the pound, man. You need to stop the love-fest and lead us out of here."

I had forgotten all about our mission. I quickly assembled the troops, and then broke them into smaller groups of three. I would lead the big, old boy dogs, Shaq would take the smaller boys and Kobe, of course, would lead the girls.

"Come on," I said once everybody was in place. "We are going to lead you to the Interstate, which is about one mile from here."

"Ok, essay," I heard Taco bark from Shaq's group. "But can we go to What a Taco first?"

CHAPTER 3

I took my group first, and then Kobe followed with her group and Shaq's gang followed all of us. I have to admit that I didn't know where we were going.

"I have a very famous nose," I said as I stopped and yelled back to everyone. "Just follow along. I won't let you down."

We walked across a lot of rocks and brush for what seemed like an hour before we came to a store with a lot of gas pumps outside. It had a giant K on top of it with a circle around the K.

"Does anybody need anything?" I asked as we all stopped about 100 feet away from the store.

"I need some burritos," yelled Taco.

"No burritos," I yelled back. "Do you need any water or napkins for the bottom of your feet? We don't have money, so we can't go in the store and buy food."

"What is money?" yelled Bruiser in a gravelly voice.

That was funny. That was the kind of question I used to ask Harley, one of my best friends in the neighborhood. I miss Harley. He could lead us all right back home.

"Never mind," I yelled. "I will turn the hose on outside and go dig into the trash and see what we can round up for food and napkins."

I went over to the water spout and tried to turn it with both front paws. It wouldn't budge. I tried to bite it. No luck.

"Let me handle this," Bruiser said.

The big bulldog lifted up his right paw and turned it on with one quick twitch. Water was flying everywhere out of the hose that obviously had a lot of holes in it.

"There you go," Bruiser said.

The dogs were going crazy. They obviously were thirsty. By the time Bruiser turned the water off, we looked like Alvin and the Chipmunks instead of dogs.

"Yo, C-Man," Taco yelled. "When are we going to eat?"

I went over to the big trash can and tried to jump up and in. No luck. Shaq tried to jump in. No luck. Then Bruiser had an idea.

"I will stand here," Bruiser said, "and all of you start piling on my back. It is like building a tower. Once you get to the top, jump in."

Kobe wanted to go last.

"I don't want any of you boys jumping on my back," she said.

I agreed. We started climbing one on top of the other. Soon, Kobe was near the top. But she didn't want to jump in.

Girls.

"I am not going in there," Kobe yelled down. "It is too gross."

"Come on, Kobe," I said. "We need to find a little bit of food before we start the rest of our journey."

Kobe held her nose with her left paw and dived in the dumpster. She came up with chicken bones, half-eaten hamburgers, a few French Fries, tons of napkins and even some old burritos.

"That a way to go, Kobe," Shaq yelled. "I knew we could count on you."

Kobe drew a big smile to her face and then started tossing out the food all over the ground. As soon as something touched the cement, it was a fight to see who could eat it first.

"Now, this is a fiesta, man," Taco said.

After we finished eating, Bruiser turned on the hose again. We got some water, cleaned ourselves up and headed back toward the Interstate.

"How much further?" asked Leprechaun, who obviously was not a walker. "My front paws feel like I have been walking on hot coals."

Honestly, I didn't know how much further. And I didn't know how I was going to tell most of the dogs good-bye when we got to the Interstate.

"It shouldn't be too far now," I said. "Once we get to the Interstate, you will feel like you are half-way home."

I don't know how many dogs believed me. Heck, I didn't believe myself. But it sounded good. So we took off walking again.

CHAPTER 4

We trudged about 300 feet when the road started to turn into a big hill. We couldn't see over the hill, but we could hear the roar of cars.

"Come on, guys!" I shouted. "I know the Interstate is just over this hill."

"What about What a Taco?" shouted Taco.

"Ignore him," Kobe said as she ran up toward me. "He is loco."

I had another idea. I wanted to line everyone up single file so we could look like we were on a walk for "Animal Rights." I saw that on television once with Tyler. Dogs need some respect, too, you know.

But when I turned around, Taco had turned the other two packs of dogs into Dance Party USA. They were hopping, skipping and jumping around like it was New Year's Eve.

"Hey," I yelled. "Do you guys want to get home or not?"

Suddenly, everybody stopped. They looked at me, tilted their heads and then all sat down on the spot.

"That is better," I said. "Now, we have to walk single file so the cars don't hit us and we look like we are on a mission."

Shaq gathered his troops and Kobe rounded up hers. All the dogs did exactly what I asked, except, of course, Taco and Bruiser.

"What are you guys doing?" I yelled back.

They both looked up and smiled. They had found a bag of old donuts on the road. Taco's face looked like a chocolate glazed donut. Bruiser chose the jelly filled ones.

"Are you two about done?" I asked.

"Wait just a minute, Jose," Taco said. "Aw, shucks, you guys just go ahead. We will catch up to you. These donuts are so good, man."

I couldn't leave Taco and Bruiser. They were pretty funny, I had to admit. So we waited. And waited. And waited.

Finally, Bruiser yelled: "Take us to the Interstate, oh gracious leader."

I shook my head, lined up my group single file and started to walk up the steep hill. To my surprise, the other groups followed. When we reached the top of the hill, we could see the road leading to the Interstate.

But the Interstate still had to be a mile away.

"Hey, Celtic," Leprechaun said. "My feet are killing me again. I thought you said the Interstate was right over this hill."

"Yea, Jose," Taco chimed in. "It looks like the Interstate is in Mexico, man."

Kobe and Shaq walked over to me. The three of us were going to have to come up with a plan to not only keep walking, but keep the dogs believing this was the right thing to do.

"Celtic," Shaq said. "We trust you. Let us say something to them."

"Be my guest, brother," I said. It was the first time I really grasped the thought of having a brother. It was nice.

"Hey, everybody," Shaq yelled in a very stern voice. "Celtic has been on many adventures and survived every one of them. He knows where he is going and what he is doing. We have to listen to him."

The other dogs cowered down. Taco put his paws over his head. Bruiser laid right down on his stomach.

"That ought to do it," Shaq said.

"I sure hope so," Kobe added. "That Interstate still looks pretty far away."

CHAPTER 5

The dogs were amazingly quiet and well-behaved as we trudged on.

I couldn't figure out if they were still scared of Shaq, or if they thought we were leading them back to the Dog Pound.

Taco finally answered my question.

"Hey, Celtic Man," Taco said in his best Spanish accent. "What is going to happen when we finally reach this Interstate?"

I didn't have the heart to tell him that most of the dogs were going to be turned loose to find their way home, so I tried to ignore him.

Then Leprechaun chimed in.

"Uh, Celtic," Leprechaun said. "Do you have some kind of magic wand that you can wave and take us all back home? I am getting very homesick on this journey."

I finally had to confess.

"Ok," I barked in my loudest one-year-old voice. "Everybody listen."

The whole clan stopped. Well, almost the whole clan. Bruiser was twirling around trying to catch his tail. Taco was trying to catch Bruiser.

"Here is the deal," I continued on, trying to ignore Taco and Bruiser's three-ring circus. "When we get to the Interstate, most of you are going to be on your own."

Taco and Bruiser stopped twirling. Leprechaun started crying. The rest of the dogs looked like a bunch of whipped puppies.

"I know this sounds harsh," I said, "but I don't know where you live. You have to follow your nose and believe in yourself.

"I have a wise old dog on my street named Parker," I continued. "He taught me one thing. Always believe in yourself. I know that you guys can find your way home. Just start sniffing and keep believing."

Taco and Bruiser didn't believe anything.

"Hey, Celtic, man," Taco said, "you can't leave me alone. I am scared of my own shadow, essay."

"Yea, C," added Bruiser. "I might look big and tough, but I don't like being by myself. I am afraid of the dark."

I asked Taco and Bruiser where they lived.

"In Hidden Lakes subdivision," they both said at once.

I couldn't believe it.

"Me, too," said Leprechaun, who obviously was listening in on the conversation.

Then, I had an idea.

"Do any of you other dogs live in Hidden Lakes subdivision?" I barked to the three groups. Nobody said a thing. "OK, I said. When we get to the Interstate, Taco, Bruiser, Leprechaun, Shaq, Kobe and me are going one way and the rest of you are going your own way."

I heard gruffly barks, shaking, scratching and a lot of sniffing. But nobody spoke up. I guess everybody finally agreed to the plan.

"Here we are," I said after about 10 more minutes of walking. "I am very proud I could rescue all of you from the Dog Pound. Now, make me proud and find your way home."

I gave each dog a hug and a sniff. When the last one finally trudged off, the six of us were left to try and find Hidden Lakes subdivision.

We knew it was a long way off. But we really didn't know what was in store for us.

CHAPTER 6

We had reached the Interstate. Now, the trick was crossing the Interstate. Coby taught me to make sure and look both ways. But these cars were going fast. And there was no break in sight.

"Wow," I said to Shaq, who was rapidly becoming my best friend. "This might take a while."

"That's OK, C," he said. "Now that we are all together, we are in no hurry. We just want to get home safe."

Just then Taco stuck out his right paw and Bruiser stuck out his left paw.

"What are you guys doing?" I asked them.

"We are hitchhiking," Taco said with a hilarious laugh.

"Yea, Celtic," Bruiser said. "Maybe we can catch a ride to Hidden Lakes."

Those two were going to drive me crazy. But I had to admit they were a lot of fun. And I do love to have fun.

"Put your paws down and come on," I said. "We have a little break here if we can all run as fast as we can."

I sprinted across four lanes of traffic. Shaq and Kobe followed, and Leprechaun practically bunny-hopped like a kangaroo over to the other side of the road.

But when I turned around, Taco and Bruiser were still on the other side. A cab driver had stopped to give them a ride.

"Hey, Celtic, look at this cool car man," Taco yelled as they climbed in the cab.

A couple seconds later, they were getting out of the taxi.

"Costs money," Bruiser said. "The driver told us to give him $10 or get out. We had to get out."

I felt sorry for the two peas in a pod. But I was glad they were back with the group.

"What now?" asked Taco.

"We walk," I said. "Just stay off the road. We are going to have to cut through a lot of parking lots, stores and fast food joints, but I know this is the right direction."

Taco drew a big smile to his face. What a Taco was no more than 100 yards in front of us.

"Please, Celtic," he begged. "You have to take me to Taco Bell. They have a new 18-layer burrito, man."

I had never heard of such a thing. But Bruiser said it was true.

"Yea," Bruiser said. "I saw it advertised on TV. It looks good. I could eat about 13 of them."

"But you don't have any money," I said.

"But they throw away the leftovers in the trash can," Taco said. "I know. I love digging in trash cans."

He was right. There were plenty of leftovers in the big trash can. I had never seen a little Chihuahua eat so much food in my life.

Bruiser didn't eat quite as much, but his stomach was so bloated that he had to lie down.

"I don't feel so good," Bruiser said. "I need a belly rub."

I love belly rubs, I thought to myself. I miss Tyler. He would give me a belly rub. We had to keep moving.

"OK, guys, up and at them," I said. "We still have a long way to go. And I'm sure our families are worried sick about us."

Leprechaun kind of hung his head.

"I don't really have a family," admitted the Irish Setter. "I lied about living in Hidden Lakes. I just didn't want to be alone. Do you think I could come live with you Celtic?"

"Sure," I said. "I am sure Tyler won't mind."

But Dad might.

CHAPTER 7

After cleaning out the dumpster by What a Taco, we started to walk along the side of a four-lane road.

"Where are we going now, C-Dog?" asked Taco.

I was following my nose. I had been this way before. There were all sorts of smells I recognized.

"Trust me," I told Taco. "I know where I am."

Kobe and Shaq weren't so sure.

"Uh, Celtic," Shaq said. "This is a pretty busy street and there are no houses in site."

"Yea, brother," Kobe added. "All I see is road, fast food joints and lots of stoplights. I don't know how much more of this I can take. I am definitely going to need my toenails done."

"Have patience," I said. "This is a marathon, not a sprint. It is going to take a while."

The group all groaned. But there was one groan missing. Bruiser was gone.

"Where is Bruiser?" I asked.

Everybody just shook their head. Then, Leprechaun spoke up.

"He said something about cruising over to Sonic," Leprechaun said.

Sure enough, I looked across the street, and Bruiser was putting his paw on one of the order buttons at Drinks & More.

"Bruiser!," I screamed over the traffic. "What in the world are you doing?"

"I am thirsty," he said. "I want one of those Route 36 cokes."

How did he know about a Route 44 drink, I thought. Do all dads go to Drinks & More and order Route 36 drinks?

"You don't have any money," I said.

"But I have my health," Bruiser barked back.

When the lady came on the speaker, Bruiser barked out "Route 36 Coke." Unbelievably, she brought him his drink, petted him on the head and went back inside.

"People love Bulldogs," Bruiser said.

We all looked at each other, looked both ways, and then ran across the street to Drinks & More. We had Bruiser order two slushes, an ice cream sundae and apple slices.

"Wow, Bruiser," Taco said with a mouth stained with melted ice cream. "You sure know how to throw a fiesta."

Bruiser just smiled, and strutted around like a bow-legged peacock. He was pleased with himself. I had to admit, I enjoyed the apple slices, too.

"Okay, gang," I said after my last bite of apple slice. "We have got to get moving if we are going to make it home before dark."

Taco was jumping around like he was on a pogo stick.

"I don't know why, but I always get so excited after eating ice cream," Taco said.

Bruiser was passed out on the ground again. Leprechaun, Shaq and Kobe were making friends with all the kids at Drinks & More.

"Hey, everybody," I said. "Did you hear me? We have to keep walking. And I don't want to cross the road again. We are going to walk on this side now. And that is enough food."

The group finally came together. Taco was still like a ping-pong ball bouncing on the cement. And Bruiser had terrible gas. But we were ready to move on. I prayed that we didn't have any more interruptions.

CHAPTER 8

The dogs, surprisingly, did just as I told them. We stayed on the same side of the road as I continued to try and sniff my way back to Hidden Lakes.

"Now I know why they call it Hidden Lakes," I thought to myself. "Nobody can find the darned place."

After a short while, we came upon a sign. I didn't know how to read. Neither did Shaq or Kobe. And I wasn't about to ask the other two knuckleheads, Taco and Bruiser.

"The Woodlands Raiders High School," Leprechaun said.

I was stunned. Leprechaun was about the smartest stray dog I knew.

"That rings a bell," I told the other dogs. Then it hit me.

"Colton goes to Raiders High School," I said. "Let's go find him. He could take us back to Hidden Lakes."

They all looked at me and tilted their head. Finally, Bruiser spoke up.

"Who is this Colton and why is he in that school. Does he need to be trained?"

I laughed.

"No," I said. "He goes there to play football. He plays catch with me in the street. He is, well, my human big brother."

Taco started jumping around again.

"I can almost smell my casa now," he said as he started humming some Mexican tune called La Bamba. "Let's go find this Colton."

When we got to the high school, it was huge. It had to be a mile long. How were we going to find Colton in this big place, I thought?

Obviously, the other dogs thought the same thing.

"Come on, Celtic," Kobe said. "There is no way we are going to find your brother in there. It is way too big."

But I didn't want to give up. I knew we couldn't go in the front door, so we climbed in an open window by the basketball gym.

"I know Colton likes to shoot baskets, too," I said. "Maybe he is in here."

They all tilted their heads again.

"No comprende, man," Taco said.

"Yea," Bruiser added. "We don't understand."

"Follow me," I said.

When we got in the building, we saw a huge room with six baskets, a big scoreboard hanging down from the roof and benches that were piled 20 feet high.

"This looks like something on Cops," Taco said.

"Yea," added Bruiser. "When the Dog Catcher busted me, he threw me in a big room like this one. But it didn't have any baskets. It had iron bars."

"Hush up you two," I said. "You want somebody to find us? Don't you know that dogs are not allowed to go to school?"

"I went to obedience school," Leprechaun said.

So, that explains it, I mumbled to myself.

"We did, too," Kobe and Shaq added at the same time.

Good grief. That puts me in a league with Taco and Bruiser, I thought.

About that time, we saw a big man pushing a broom and a pail of water.

"Hey, Bruiser," Taco said. "Call that guy over here. You need a bath, essay."

Bruiser laughed. He did stink. But this was no time for baths. We quickly darted behind the bleachers.

"What are we going to do, Celtic?" Shaq asked.

I really didn't know. But I was sure we were about to find out.

"Just sit tight while I think," I told Shaq.

The man seemed like he took an hour mopping the entire floor before he finally left. Once he did, Taco and Bruiser decided to go skiing.

"Wheeeee!!!," Taco said as he ran and slid on the still very wet floor. "This is fun."

"Try it on your belly," Bruiser added as he scooted across the floor on his big chest. "It is unbelievable."

Pretty soon, we had turned the basketball floor into a skating rink. I even went out there and acted like I was water skiing on my back paws.

"OK, gang," I said, laughing. "We have to get serious. We have to find Colton. If we don't, it is going to be a long trip home."

"I am home," said Taco, who had found a half-eaten taco in the garbage can inside the gym. "This is my new home."

CHAPTER 9

We found a door leading out of the gym and slowly peeked around the corner to see if the coast was clear. There were a few kids wandering around, but if we were quick, we decided we could make it to the library, which was about 15 yards away.

"On my signal, everybody dash toward the room with all the books," I said.

The dogs nodded.

"Go!" I said.

I had never seen Bruiser move so fast. He got there first, followed by Shaq, Kobe, Leprechaun and me.

"Where is Taco?" I asked from inside the library.

"He had to get a drink to wash down his taco," Bruiser said.

Sure enough, Taco was at the water fountain trying to jump up and get a drink.

"Are you crazy, man?" I screamed. "Get over here."

Taco trotted to the library with a disgusted look on his face.

"That taco was not good, man," he said. "It gave me indigestion."

"Serves you right," Kobe said. "Quit eating out of the trash can all the time."

"Quiet, you two," I said. "We have got to keep moving. We have got to find the football room. I know Colton plays football."

We waited a minute, saw the coast was clear, and then trotted down the main hall until we saw a big office.

"What does it say on the office," I asked Leprechaun.

"Head Football Coach," Leprechaun answered.

"We are almost there," I said.

We went into the office, but there were no football players and no head coach. The room was barely big enough to fit all of us.

"How do they play football in here?" Kobe asked.

"Yea," Shaq added. "One good hit and the whole place comes down."

"They play outside," I said. "At each end of the field, they have two huge things that look like forks."

"Then what are we doing inside?" Leprechaun asked.

Good question. We had to get back outside and find the football field.

"Leprechaun," I said. "You are one smart dog."

Taco and Bruiser just laughed.

"He is not so smart," Taco said. "If he were that smart, we would be home by now."

"Don't listen to them," I told Leprechaun. "We will find the football field and then Colton will take us home. We will see what they have to say then."

We walked out of the "Head Football Coach's" office and headed back toward the gym. Once in the gym, we slipped back out the window and saw two huge forks about 200 yards away.

"There is the football field," I screamed.

We all sprinted toward the field. When we arrived, we went to the bleachers and sat down.

"All we have to do is wait," I said. "Pretty soon, Colton will be out here playing football."

"I hope so," Bruiser said. "If not, I am giving up on this mission and heading back to Drinks & More. I could go for a chili cheese dog."

"Now, Bruiser is a smart dog," Taco said. "Chili and cheese are the best things to put on a taco."

CHAPTER 10

We waited for what seemed like an entire day before we saw some boys come running toward the football field in something that looked like a space suit.

"Who are those guys?" Kobe asked.

"Those are football players," I said.

"They look like Martians to me," Kobe said with a laugh. "What is that thing on their head?"

Colton had never worn one of those when he made me chase the football in the street. But I saw one hanging in his room.

"I think it is called a helmet," I said. "Colton has an old one from when he played when he was a little boy. I think it is a weapon."

The other dogs looked at me and tilted their heads.

"A weapon? Are you kidding me, essay? Are we going to see a big fight?," Taco asked.

"We might," I said. "And I don't want to see Colton get hurt. We have to find him fast."

But all the guys had weapons on their head. And, with their weapons on, I couldn't tell who Colton was.

"I have to go out and start sniffing the players. I can't tell who Colton is," I told the group. "The rest of you stay here and don't look suspicious."

As I ran on the field, several of the guys wanted to pet me. But I had no time for games. I had to find my brother.

"Have you seen Colton?" I barked at Colton's friends, Travis and Ryan. They didn't understand me. They wanted to wrestle. They couldn't believe I was at football practice.

"Have you seen Colton," I barked again.

Finally, Ryan yelled: "Colton, your dog is here."

Colton took his weapon off and came running over to me. He was so excited to see me. And I was so excited to see him.

"Where have you been, boy?" he said. "We thought you were gone forever. Tyler has been crying like crazy."

I tried to tell him, but only Tyler can understand me. I did get him to notice the other dogs. He told me to go wait with them and he would give me a ride home after practice.

"Thank you so much, Colton," I said as I licked his face over and over again. "I love you so much."

I ran over to the other dogs and told them we had to wait patiently until practice was over.

"Why can't we go out there and play?" asked Bruiser.

"We don't have weapons," I said. "Besides, those guys are too big."

"But they would never catch us," Leprechaun said.

He had a point there. Tyler and Colton were fast, but they could never catch me.

"After practice, we can run around the football field a little bit," I promised. "But we have to stay here until they are done."

A couple hours later, we all took turns racing from one end of the football field to the other. Bruiser and Taco were way out of shape. They stopped after two trips.

"I need water," Bruiser barked.

"I need Tacos and Beans," yelled Taco.

Leprechaun, Kobe, Shaq and me kept right on running. The grass felt so good under our feet. We felt like we were free. We felt safe. We knew we were finally going home.

"Come on, Celtic," Colton yelled as he came out of the school in his normal clothes. "It is time to go home."

All the dogs followed me over to the car. We all piled in the back seat.

"Is this a limousine?" Bruiser asked.

I laughed. I had heard that somewhere before. Oh, yea, my cousin Benny.

"No," I said, "but this is the car that is going to take us home."

Colton dropped off Kobe and Shaq first. Their parents were so happy they were crying. I was crying, too. I wanted to keep in touch with them.

"Celtic, we live right around the corner from you," Shaq said. "You can come over and swim any time."

Taco and Bruiser were next. It turned out they only lived two houses from each other.

"Hey, Bruiser," Taco said. "I have always been afraid of you, essay. But now I want you to come over all the time. You are my home boy."

Finally, we arrived at our house. I sprinted in to see Tyler. He burst into tears. Mom and Dad also started crying. It was one of the happiest moments of my life.

Leprechaun, meanwhile, sat back and watched. He had been a stray all his life. I didn't want him to be a stray anymore.

"Who is this, Celtic?" Tyler asked me.

I told him it was Leprechaun and that he was a stray.

"Dad," Tyler said. "Can we keep the other dog. I think he is a stray."

Dad looked at the big Irish Setter and laughed.

"Why not," he said. "He can't be any more trouble than Celtic, can he?"

Leprechaun just smiled. Maybe he can.

Printed in the United States
By Bookmasters